Adapted by Jasmine Jones
Based on the series created by Terri Minsky
Part One is based on a teleplay written
by Melissa Gould.
Part Two is based on a teleplay written
by Jeremy J. Bargiel & Nina G. Bargiel.

New York

Copyright © 2004 Disney Enterprises, Inc.

All rights reserved. No part of this book may be reproduced
or transmitted in any form or by any means, electronic or
mechanical, including photocopying, recording, or by any
information storage and retrieval system, without written
permission from the publisher. For information address
Disney Press, 114 Fifth Avenue, New York, New York 10011-5690.

Printed in the United States of America

First Edition
1 3 5 7 9 10 8 6 4 2

Library of Congress Catalog Card Number: 2003112226

ISBN 0-7868-4551-1
For more Disney Press fun, visit www.disneybooks.com
Visit DisneyChannel.com

If you purchased this book without a cover, you should be aware
that this book is stolen property. It was reported as "unsold and
destroyed" to the publisher, and neither the author nor the
publisher has received any payment for this "stripped" book.

Lizzie McGUiRE

PART ONE

CHAPTER ONE

"**N**o, no, no," Lizzie McGuire said as her best friend, Miranda Sanchez, danced to the pop music that was blasting from the CD player. When Lizzie and Miranda's other best friend, David "Gordo" Gordon, had announced that he wanted to shoot a music video, the girls had jumped at the chance to dance in it. They'd been working on their choreography for the past three days, and it was really starting to come together. Lizzie swung her right arm across her body with staccato rhythm. "It's Britney, Britney, Janet," Lizzie said, demonstrating. Then she did a funky head move. "And then, J.Lo."

Miranda shook her head. "Wrong," she replied, then busted into her own order of the dance moves. "It's Britney, *Janet*, Janet—"

"I'm hearing music. . . ." Gordo said as he walked into Lizzie's living room with a tray full of snacks. He really has an unnatural ability to sniff out junk food in my family's kitchen, Lizzie thought as she eyed the munchies. I mean, where did those Cheese Puffs come from?

"I'm seeing dancers . . . getting a whiff of that sweet smell of success," Gordo continued as he plopped the tray onto the coffee table.

"I need to refuel," Miranda said, diving toward the snacks. She shoved a chocolate-chip cookie into her mouth, and Gordo flopped down on the couch.

"Me, too," Lizzie agreed, lunging at the Cheese Puffs. Then her eye fell on something even better. "Peanut butter!" she cried, grabbing the jar and a soup spoon.

Miranda wolfed down another cookie as Lizzie licked her spoonful of peanut butter. Yum!

Gordo shook his head as he watched the girls scarf down the goodies. "Man, you guys eat *a lot*!" He took a bite of a Cheese Puff.

Lizzie ignored him. "Ooh, I should get some pretzels!" she said to Miranda. Lizzie thought that pretzels dipped in peanut butter were *deelish*!

"You guys think you could stop stuffing your faces long enough for us to finish rehearsal?" Gordo asked.

We're girls. We can multitask.

"Gordo, just 'cause we're eating doesn't mean we're not rehearsing," Miranda said through a mouthful of chocolate-chip cookie.

Lizzie nodded in agreement, tossing her long blond hair over her shoulder. She and Miranda had been dancing for two hours straight! Who cared about a spoonful-of-peanut-butter break?

"You guys, this music video needs to be taken seriously." Gordo leaned forward on the couch to drive his point home. "I'm branching out. Expanding my repertoire."

"Yeah, it'll look good on your school record," Miranda agreed, sending cookie crumbs flying. She pointed to herself and turned to Lizzie. "Ours, too, Lizzie."

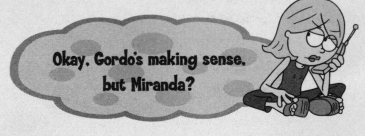

Okay, Gordo's making sense, but Miranda?

Lizzie raised her eyebrows. Since when did Miranda worry about school records? She was just about to ask Miranda what she was talking about when Lizzie's annoying little brother, Matt, walked into the living room with his best friend, Lanny. The good thing about Lanny, as far as Lizzie was concerned, was that he never said a word. This was more than she could say for her little brother, who unfortunately always seemed to have something weird to share.

Like right now, for example. He was standing there in a black turtleneck and a goofy-looking beret, staring at Lizzie, and she just knew that he was going to say something irritating. It was only a matter of time. He gaped at her, and held up his finger and thumb in an L shape, as though he were framing her face with his hand. Lanny held up his thumb and nodded.

Lizzie narrowed her eyes at Matt. "What are you staring at?"

"Watch a *real* artist at work," Matt said in a bored voice. He lowered his eyelids and smirked at her, then took a massive sketch pad from Lanny and began to scribble away on it like a madman.

"Whatever you're doing, stop!" Lizzie commanded, folding her arms across her chest.

But Matt didn't listen . . . as usual. His hand just kept flying across the page. Finally, he looked up at his sister and flipped his sketch pad over. "Behold," he said, holding up a charcoal drawing of Lizzie.

The picture on his pad actually kind of looked like her—sort of. That is, it looked the way Lizzie would have looked if her mother had been a rectangle and her father a trapezoid. The drawing was abstract . . . but you could still make out the resemblance. "I call this one, *Girl Who Makes Me Hurl*," Matt said in a haughty voice.

Lizzie planted her hands on her hips. "Well, I call this one *Brother About to Run for His Life.*"

Matt scrambled out of the room, and Lizzie dashed after him.

Miranda frowned and then called out to Lizzie, "Could you get those pretzels while you're up?"

"I studied, I quizzed, I made diagrams!" Miranda raged as she stormed over to join Lizzie and Gordo at Lizzie's locker. "And for what? A no good, lousy *B*!" Miranda scowled at the offending paper in disgust, and flipped two of her four dark braids over her shoulder. Her nostrils flared as she held the paper up for Lizzie to inspect. "That could mean the difference between 'President for you on line two, Ms. Sanchez' or 'You want fries with that?'" Miranda made a sour face as she envisioned her future working behind the deep fryer.

Lizzie hugged her notebook against her chest. "Okay, so you got a B on a science test," she said in her best What's-the-Big-Deal? voice. "A B is *above average*." Lizzie never got freaked out about anything that could be considered above average.

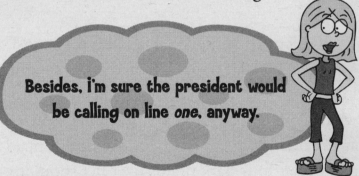

Besides, i'm sure the president would be calling on line *one*, anyway.

"There'll be plenty of tests for you to get an A on," Gordo said encouragingly. "The school year's hardly over."

Lizzie resisted the impulse to roll her eyes. Why does Gordo have to remind me how long we have before summer vacation? she thought as she shut her locker.

Miranda sighed as the three friends started down the hall toward their next class. "It's just, my dad was a straight-A student, my mom was president of the Latin Club. I try so hard and still I end up 'above average.'" Miranda was speaking in a tone of voice that made "above average" sound like "pathetic loser." She stared at the floor as she went on. "For once I'd like to be A—excellent."

"Excellent?" Gordo repeated, grinning. "I'll show you excellent." He reached into his book bag and pulled out some photos. "These are the stills I shot of you guys the other day." Gordo handed the stack of photos to Lizzie.

"Oh, cool," Lizzie said warmly as she looked down at the top photo. It was an awesome shot of Miranda, who had just hit a cool dance move and was smiling brilliantly into the camera. "I didn't know you shot black-and-whites."

"Yeah, well, I'm experimenting with different tones," Gordo said, waving his hand dismissively. "You know, for the video."

"Ooh, cutting edge." Miranda waggled her eyebrows. "I like it."

Lizzie handed the photos over to Miranda, so that her friend could see how great she looked. But Miranda took one look at herself in the shot, and her jaw dropped open. Then she gasped.

"What's wrong?" Lizzie asked.

"I . . ." Miranda stammered. She looked up at her friends with wide eyes, clearly horrified. "You . . ."

"Okay, okay," Gordo said quickly, "so I won't shoot it in black-and-white."

"It's not that," Miranda insisted, turning back to the photos. "It's just . . . how come no one has ever told me I have, like, six chins?"

Lizzie grabbed the photos back from Miranda, thoroughly confused. She looked at the shot. Six chins? Lizzie thought. What is Miranda talking about? She looks amazing in this snapshot.

"Because you only have one?" Lizzie answered.

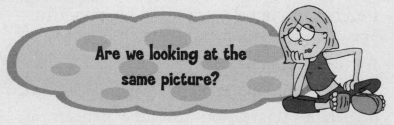

Are we looking at the same picture?

Miranda snatched the photos back from Lizzie. "And my arms!" Miranda wailed. "They're so big!"

"What are you talking about, Miranda?" Lizzie demanded. "You look *great* in that picture."

"I think you're overreacting," Gordo said reasonably.

"Overreacting?" Miranda demanded. "Overreacting? We're about to shoot a video! You do know the camera adds ten pounds, don't you?" Miranda was so upset, she was practically shouting.

Okay, be reassuring, Lizzie told herself. She really didn't understand why her friend was freaking out, but she wanted to be supportive. "Don't worry," Lizzie said. "We'll wear black. It's very slimming."

"That won't be enough!" Miranda looked desperate. "Have you seen the dancers in those videos? Not only are they gorgeous, they're tiny!" She said, stressing the word "tiny" and holding her finger and thumb a half inch apart. "I'm not tiny, or gorgeous!" Miranda clenched her teeth.

Hello? it's called airbrushing. Nobody in the real world looks like that.

"Maybe you're right, Gordo," Miranda said finally. "Maybe I do eat too much."

Gordo looked shocked. "I never said you eat too much."

Lizzie gave him a sideways glance. Was it fair that they lived in a universe in which boys forgot an insult a split second after it happened, while girls remembered everything? "Yeah, you did," Lizzie pointed out. "Yesterday."

The whole scene flashed through her mind—she and Miranda pigging out on peanut butter and cookies, and Gordo telling them that they sure ate a lot. Way to be tactful, Gordo, Lizzie thought, rolling her eyes.

"That's it," Miranda said, pursing her lips.

She slapped the photos into Gordo's hands. "I'm going on a diet."

Lizzie watched Miranda storm down the hall. Was she *serious*? Miranda didn't need to go on a diet . . . she just needed to get a grip!

CHAPTER TWO

Mrs. McGuire staggered into the living room, where her husband was tapping away on the computer keyboard. "Sam, honey?" she said in a weak voice as she sat down on the couch.

"Huh?" Mr. McGuire continued typing.

"I just got off the phone with Matt's school." Mrs. McGuire looked dazed.

"Oh, no," Mr. McGuire said with a groan. "What'd he do this time?"

Mrs. McGuire shook her head. She really

could not believe the conversation she had just had with Matt's principal. She had actually hung up, and then called back to ask if it had been a practical joke, but the principal had assured her that the phone call had been 100 percent for real. "Just brace yourself."

Mr. McGuire looked up at his wife, very concerned. Matt had done some pretty weird things. For Mrs. McGuire to be reacting like this was really saying something!

"He's okay, isn't he?" Mr. McGuire asked.

"Oh, yeah." Mrs. McGuire nodded. "He's okay. I have to lie down from the shock of it all." She flopped weakly against a mountain of couch pillows.

Mr. McGuire leaned in toward his wife, obviously worried. "Did he sneak into kindergarten class and take a nap again?"

Mrs. McGuire shook her head. *That* had been a weird phone call—Matt had managed to stay in the kindergarten class all though story time, and snack time as well. But it wasn't half as strange as what she had heard today. "No."

"Did he eat all the ice-cream sandwiches in the cafeteria like he did last week?" Mr. McGuire asked. Last Tuesday, Matt had sneaked into the school cafeteria while the lunch ladies were on a coffee break and emptied out the freezer. His allowance was being garnished for at least the next one hundred thirty-seven weeks to cover the cost of *that* one!

"No." Mrs. McGuire let out a stream of air through pursed lips.

"Tell me he didn't pretend to be the P.E. substitute?" Mr. McGuire begged. He stood up and walked over to his wife, planting his hands on his hips. A month earlier, Matt had taken over the third graders' physical education class. He had made everyone do a thousand jumping jacks, then announced that the class would play a game of dodge ball, and that the losers would receive a failing grade in the class—for the year.

"Sit." Mrs. McGuire patted the seat next to her on the couch.

"Okay," Mr. McGuire said as he sat down beside his wife.

Mrs. McGuire looked at her husband over the tops of her rectangular glasses. "Apparently, he has the potential to be the Picasso of his generation," she said slowly.

"Picasso?" Mr. McGuire's forehead crinkled in confusion. "Our Matt? Matt McGuire? Are you sure there isn't another Matt in his class?"

"Sam," Mrs. McGuire said patiently, "we'll have to encourage him. Artists are very sensitive."

"Sensitive?" Mr. McGuire shook his head. "Matt eats mud."

Mrs. McGuire thought about that. It was

true. But on the other hand, all geniuses were pretty weird, weren't they?

Lizzie finished a spoonful of chocolate pudding while Miranda added the final touches to her folded paper fortune-teller. They were sitting at their usual table on the school's patio, eating lunch. That is, Lizzie and Gordo were eating. *Miranda* was wrapped up in her fortune-teller project.

Gordo cocked an eyebrow at Miranda. "Tell me again why you're doing this?" he asked, gesturing at the folded paper with his plastic fork.

"So I can tell our fortunes," Miranda replied as she placed the fortune-teller on her fingers and held it out to Lizzie.

"But *you're* the one writing them," Gordo pointed out. "It doesn't count."

"Why not?" Lizzie demanded. As far as she

was concerned, Miranda was just as qualified to tell the future as anyone else. Just because she wrote optimistic things inside of her fortune-teller didn't mean that she had to be *wrong*, did it? Lizzie pointed to a fortune flap.

Gordo flashed Lizzie an impatient look and waved at the fortune-teller. "Well, because she's not really predicting the future."

Miranda peeled back the flap above the fortune Lizzie had chosen. "'You will marry Ethan Craft,'" Miranda read, smiling at Lizzie triumphantly. Ethan Craft was the biggest hottie at Hillridge Junior High, and both Lizzie and Miranda had major crushes on him. Miranda looked up at Gordo. "It doesn't get much realer than that, Gordo," she told him in a proud voice.

Gordo shrugged and picked at the food on his plate. "At least, *you* are in a better mood than you were this morning."

"Yeah. See, Miranda?" Lizzie chirped. "Getting a B is not that bad."

"Yeah, I'm totally over it." Miranda gave Lizzie a quick smile, and then looked down at her paper fortune. "I'll just work harder for the next test."

Gordo watched Miranda fiddle with the fortune-teller. "How come you're not eating anything?" he asked her.

"Oh, I, um, I ate a really big breakfast." Miranda held out the paper to Lizzie again. Since when does Miranda let a big breakfast stand in the way of lunch? Lizzie wondered. "Okay, pick," she commanded.

"Two," Lizzie said, pointing to a new flap. Miranda flipped the fortune-teller back and forth between her fingers, then peeled back the fortune and squealed. "You will marry Ethan Craft!"

Lizzie let out a shriek of delight. This was

the best paper fortune-teller ever! It was frighteningly accurate.

Okay, so maybe it is just a stupid paper fortune, but i like what it's saying!

Gordo rolled his eyes. "They all say that."

The smile dropped off Miranda's face. "I'll just make another one." She pulled out a new piece of paper from her notebook and started to fold it.

"Miranda, are you sure you don't want some of my . . ." Lizzie held up her plate, which was filled with a congealed mass of something yellow, with small green-and-red chunks in it. It had been the lunch special. "Uh, you know," Lizzie said uncertainly, "whatever this is?"

"Ow!" Miranda said suddenly, looking down at her finger. "Ooh, paper cut. I better go run my finger under cold water." She gathered up her books. "I'll see you guys later. And don't be late after school. We have a lot of dancing to do." Miranda hurried away from the lunch patio, as though her paper cut needed immediate and *serious* medical attention.

Gordo turned to Lizzie. "I don't think I've ever seen Miranda skip a meal."

Lizzie shook her head dismissively. "She said she had a really big breakfast. . . ."

"She *also* said she's going on a diet," Gordo pointed out. "I didn't think she meant *starvation* diet."

Starvation diet? Puh-lease.

Lizzie shook her head. "Miranda is so not like that."

Gordo seemed to think about that for a moment. "Yeah, I guess you're right."

"I mean, she may not have gotten an A on the science test, but she's still not dumb," Lizzie went on. Then an image popped into her mind—the look on Miranda's face when she had seen the photo of herself. Miranda had acted like that single photo was the greatest tragedy of her life. It had really been strange—and completely unlike Miranda. "At least," Lizzie added after a moment, suddenly worried about her friend, "I hope not."

CHAPTER THREE

"Okay," Matt directed from his place behind a giant easel, "a little to the left . . . Now tilt your chin up. . . . Okay, lower your left eyelid slightly. . . ." He gestured with his paintbrush. "Perfect! Now don't move a muscle."

Lanny held the uncomfortable pose, perched on a stool in the McGuires' backyard. He didn't utter a word of complaint. He just remained his usual silent self.

Matt dipped his brush in blue paint and splattered it across the canvas . . . and across a nearby plant. He chose a new color, and attacked the canvas again, hurling paint wildly, and sending it flying across the deck— and across Lanny's face. He was getting more paint on his smock than he was on his painting!

Lanny held his pose as Matt continued to paint.

"Oh, our little artist at work," Mrs. McGuire cooed as she and her husband walked out onto the rear deck to inspect their son's latest pièce de résistance.

Mr. McGuire peered at Matt's canvas. "Let's see what you're painting there, Matt."

Lanny gasped. An expression of horror crossed his face, and he waved his arms wildly.

"It's okay, Lanny," Matt said patiently. "They don't know." He turned to his parents and explained, "I only 'show' when my work is complete."

Mrs. McGuire and her husband stared at each other for a moment.

"Oh," Mrs. McGuire said finally. "Oh. Well, in that case, we'll go. We just want you to know how proud we are of you."

Mr. McGuire nodded . . . and then he noticed the paint on the deck. He planted his hands at his waist, frowning. "And we'd be just as proud of you if you kept a little more of the paint on the canvas and a little less on the plants"—Mr. McGuire looked around— "and Lanny," he added looking at Matt's friend who was *covered* in paint.

The smile dropped from Matt's face, and the paintbrush dropped from his hand. "My inspiration," he said hoarsely. "It's . . . it's gone."

"Oh, don't be silly," Mrs. McGuire told

Lizzie smiled to herself. She was 98 percent sure her mom *hadn't* been kidding until Gordo busted her. Oh, well. At least he hadn't agreed to let Mrs. McGuire be in the video. That would have been seriously strange, Lizzie thought as she flopped into a nearby chair. She and Miranda had just run through the dance eight times straight, and Lizzie was exhausted.

"Oh!" Miranda flashed Lizzie a look of dismay as she watched her friend sink into the chair. "Come on, Lizzie. We should go over it again."

Lizzie rolled her eyes as she sat cross-legged on the chair. "Miranda, we've gone over this dance, like, a million times," she griped. Seriously, Miranda had been a total maniac about the dance all day. It was like she was on a personal mission to make sure this dance was better than anything MTV had ever seen, and she didn't want to stop until their "Janet" moves were better than the ones Janet herself did. "Ever heard of taking five?" Lizzie asked.

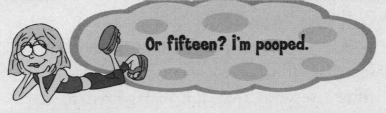

Or fifteen? i'm pooped.

"Come on, just one more time," Miranda begged, punching Lizzie on the arm playfully. "Please. It needs to be perfect."

Lizzie knew that she wasn't going to get anywhere talking to Miranda, so she tried another tactic. "Mr. Director?" she asked, turning to Gordo. "I need some help."

Gordo shrugged. "I've got no problem with perfection."

A huge grin dawned on Miranda's face.

What kind of "help" was that? Lizzie wondered as she scowled at Gordo.

"*Or* taking a break," Gordo added quickly, taking a hint from Lizzie's glare.

Lizzie sighed and looked up into Miranda's dark puppy-dog eyes.

"Please," Miranda begged again.

"Fine," Lizzie said, hauling herself out of her chair. It had been so comfortable for those fifteen seconds that she had gotten to rest. "One more time, okay?"

"Okay," Miranda said, grinning, "from the top." She gestured to Mrs. McGuire. "Cue music."

Lizzie nodded. "Yeah."

"Hey, hey, that's my line," Gordo insisted. He looked at Mrs. McGuire and waved toward the boom box. "Cue music."

Mrs. McGuire pressed the PLAY button, and Lizzie and Miranda started their routine as music began to stream from the speakers. Lizzie was just starting to get into it when

Miranda stumbled. She put her hand to her forehead and sank to the floor, shaking her head and squeezing her eyes closed.

Ohmigosh! What's the matter? Lizzie thought, totally freaked out as she rushed over to Miranda.

Mrs. McGuire stopped the music as Lizzie leaned in toward her friend. Lizzie's heart was pounding—Miranda looked so pale. She's been working herself too hard, Lizzie realized. She's making herself sick!

"Honey, are you okay?" Mrs. McGuire said as she peered into Miranda's face.

"Huh?" Miranda asked groggily. "Oh, yeah. I'm, I'm just a little woozy."

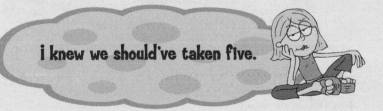

i knew we should've taken five.

"Well, you should sit down," Mrs. McGuire said gently. "Come on, we should get her some water." Mrs. McGuire helped Miranda to her feet and guided her toward the couch.

"I'll, I'll get it," Gordo said quickly, hurrying to the kitchen to get her the drink.

Miranda flopped into the deep couch pillows. She pressed a hand against her stomach, which let out a loud rumble.

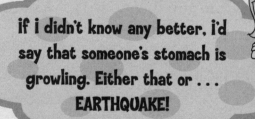

if i didn't know any better, i'd say that someone's stomach is growling. Either that or . . . EARTHQUAKE!

"Miranda, what's wrong?" Lizzie asked, sitting down on the ottoman across from her friend.

"Is it your head, or your stomach?" Mrs. McGuire asked. "Did you eat something funny?"

"Yeah, probably," Miranda said, smiling awkwardly. "I had a really big lunch."

Lizzie's eyes grew wide. Big lunch? What was Miranda talking about—that massive helping of air that she had gobbled down? She hadn't eaten anything! "Miranda," Lizzie began.

"I'm sure I'll be fine," Miranda said quickly, glaring at Lizzie.

Gordo trotted back into the living room with a large glass of water. "Here," he said, handing the glass to Miranda. "You probably just overdid it."

Miranda took the water gratefully, and nodded. "Yeah, probably," she said uncomfortably. "I'm not used to working out this hard."

"Well, you just rest here a while," Mrs. McGuire said in a soothing tone. "You guys can work on your video later."

Miranda nodded and took a sip of her water.

Okay, something serious is going on with Miranda. She's not eating, practically fainted, and just lied to my mom. It's times like these when I just have to say: HELP!

"I don't want to start panicking or anything," Gordo said nervously as he paced in front of Lizzie the next day, "but what's the deal with Miranda?" He looked at Lizzie with wide eyes for a moment, then immediately resumed pacing. Lizzie was starting to worry that he might wear out the carpet in her parents' living room.

"Okay," Lizzie said. "Well, I think that she—"

"She's obviously not herself." Gordo continued to pace, lost in his own world. "You know, with the whole diet thing. I mean, you were there, she nearly fainted rehearsing for my video. I don't know." He threw his hands in the air and drew a heavy sigh. "Maybe, maybe I should shelve the project."

Lizzie tried again. "Gordo, I think you really—"

"Or maybe you should talk to her," Gordo added quickly. "I know that the three of us are best friends, but it's just that you two have that girl thing."

"Well, you know—" Lizzie tried again to interrupt.

"I know that magazines these days are telling girls that they have to be thinner," Gordo interrupted, ignoring Lizzie. Why am I even here? she wondered as Gordo continued to pace. Gordo clearly doesn't need my help—he's freaking out all by himself.

"They're telling me I have to be more muscular," Gordo babbled on, tapping his chest, "but whatever the reason, Miranda's buying into it and I'm not. Not saying that you are, of course." He flapped a hand in Lizzie's direction. "It's just that I think you have a better handle on the situation than I would, which is why I think you should talk to her—"

"Gordo, wait." Lizzie tried to pump up the volume of her voice a little in an attempt to pierce through the dense fog of worry that seemed to be clouding Gordo's brain.

Gordo looked up at her as though he had

just noticed that she was there. He blinked. "What?"

"I want to talk to her just as bad as you do, okay?" Lizzie said. "In fact, we're going to the mall tomorrow. I'll talk to her then."

"That's, that's great," Gordo said as he sat down on the couch beside Lizzie, "because I think she needs to know that we're her friends. And that if she ever, ever needs anyone to talk to, we're her go-to peeps." Gordo punched his fist in the air. "Through thick, through thin, we'll always be there. And I gotta tell you that the whole idea of you talking to her is a huge relief, 'cause frankly, I'd have no idea what to say."

Lizzie patted Gordo on the back as he heaved a huge sigh.

Apparently, this freaking-out thing is totally contagious, Lizzie thought. I'd better go talk to Miranda before I get any worse myself.

* * *

Meanwhile, Matt and Lanny were on a quest—a quest for the perfect artistic inspiration. Matt had decided that it was time to take his artistic genius to the next level—sculpture. That was why they were combing the streets for the perfect materials. It was also why Lanny was hauling an empty red wagon behind him.

Matt paused as he walked past a garbage bin. Hmmm. What was that? He peered at the trash, and found an old bicycle wheel that he thought he could use. He rolled it into the wagon. A few moments later, Matt and Lanny walked past a pile of trash. Lanny held up a pair of blue galoshes. Matt nodded, and the galoshes went into the wagon. So did a baseball glove, an old radio, a broken toaster, six empty CD cases, a watering can, a peculiar piece of aluminum that had so many holes it looked like a slice of Swiss cheese, some pom-poms, a walker, and several other things that Matt didn't even know the names of. He grinned at Lanny, and the two friends started toward home with their now full wagon.

But, lo! No sooner had they rounded the corner than they came upon the grandest sight of all—a sign bearing the words MUNICIPAL JUNKYARD. It was a treasure trove of would-be art!

Matt's eyes grew wide at this gold mine of potential sculpture material. "Lanny," he said to his best friend, "we're going to need a bigger wagon."

CHAPTER FOUR

Lizzie and Miranda wandered into the Style Shack and headed toward the racks at the back. Lizzie couldn't really afford to buy anything there, but she was hoping that the supercool boutique would give her inspiration. She wanted to find something amazing to wear for Gordo's video. Still, Lizzie found that it was hard to keep her mind on clothes when she kept worrying about Miranda. She looked at her best friend, who was wearing her favorite black yoga pants and a white

T-shirt with red sleeves and word game puzzles printed on it. Lizzie wasn't sure if it was her imagination, or if Miranda actually looked thinner today. . . .

"Great idea to go shopping, Lizzie." Miranda sounded annoyed, as though shopping had been the worst idea in the world.

Lizzie tried not to let her friend's tone get her down. "Well, I thought we needed some new clothes for the video, right?" she asked brightly.

Miranda scoffed as she flipped through several pairs of pants on a rack. "If only I had a new body to wear them on." She crinkled her nose.

"What are you talking about?" Lizzie demanded. "You look great." She pointed to a pair of pants that Miranda was looking at and pulled them out. "Ooh! How about these?" she said cheerily.

Miranda grimaced. "Why, so my fat can hang over the top? No thanks." She turned and walked away from the pants.

Lizzie stared at her friend, frowning. What is wrong with Miranda? she wondered suddenly. Does she need glasses, or something? She looks great! This doesn't make any sense.

i'm just wondering what Miranda sees when she looks in the mirror. 'Cause it can't be what i see when i look at her.

Miranda turned her back on the clothes and peered halfheartedly at a different rack. She fiddled with the arm of a blouse.

"You know," Lizzie said suddenly, "why don't we go get some smoothies? I'm not in the mood to shop, either."

"I don't want a smoothie," Miranda said as she placed a hand over her stomach. "Besides, we just ate." She walked toward a rack of dark tops.

"Correction," Lizzie snapped. "*I* just ate. You had three French fries and a couple of bites of yogurt."

Miranda scoffed, her eyes flashing dangerously. "Thank you, Big Brother." She flipped through a rack of tops, quickly swatting through the clothes as though she were taking her aggravation out on them.

Lizzie bit her lip. Okay, so this conversation wasn't going exactly the way it had when she'd rehearsed it with Gordo. When they had gone over it, Gordo's version of "Miranda" had seen the light after about five seconds and had promised to have a huge steak for dinner and never to worry about her weight again. But the real Miranda was proving to be a much harder nut to crack. Lizzie decided to take another tack. "Miranda?" she said gently. "Do you remember that one time that you were afraid to tell me that my favorite pair of tapered, stonewashed jeans were out of style?"

"I never said that," Miranda said, not turning her attention away from the blouses on the rack, "because they were never *in* style."

"Which is exactly what you should have said when I bought them."

"Why, so you could've taken it all personal and gotten mad at me?" Miranda's eyes were wide, but she still wasn't looking at Lizzie.

"Actually, I probably would've thanked you," Lizzie admitted. "You would've spared me the weeks I spent on the Fashion Don't List."

"Good to know. I'll make a note of it." Miranda's eyes were still flashing, and her voice had an edge to it.

Lizzie sighed. She just hoped that Miranda

could actually listen to what she had to say, because it was important. "Well, there's something I want to talk to you about," Lizzie said slowly. She fiddled uncomfortably with the strap of the purse that was slung across her chest. "I'm just afraid you'll take it the wrong way."

"Okay," Miranda said. "Spill." She clenched her jaw, as though she were expecting the worst.

"You know, this whole dieting thing you're doing," Lizzie said carefully. "It makes no sense."

"Really." Miranda's eyes glittered. She folded her arms across her chest.

"It's just—Gordo didn't mean it when he said that we ate too much," Lizzie said. "I mean, you're skipping meals, Miranda You practically fainted on my living room floor, and you lied to my mom—"

"Lizzie, you're totally overreacting," Miranda said awkwardly. She backed away from her friend, retreating to the other side of the clothes rack. "Besides, it's my business."

"Miranda, we're best friends." Lizzie's voice was pleading—she just wanted her friend back. "You're obviously going through something. Why can't you just talk to me?"

Miranda stared at Lizzie for a moment. Her dark eyes were cold. "Is this the part where I'm supposed to thank you?" she asked in a flat voice.

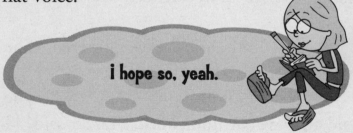

i hope so, yeah.

"I'm outie." Miranda turned on her heel and walked out of the store.

Lizzie had never felt so alone in her life.

CHAPTER FIVE

"You know, we saved seven dollars and forty-two cents," Mr. McGuire said as he and his wife walked into the house, carrying four big bags of groceries. Mr. McGuire was studying the receipt—his favorite pastime, with the exception of ceramic-gnome collecting. "I just love double coupons!" he said. He really meant it, too.

Suddenly, Mrs. McGuire stopped dead in her tracks, and Mr. McGuire bumped into her. He looked up, but it took him a moment to understand what he was seeing.

Their living room was filled with junk. Piles of twisted metal were stacked just beyond the foyer, while other objects—an old boot, a shopping cart—hung from the ceiling. At the front was a large canvas painted in vibrant colors, and behind it was a giant sculpture that featured a bicycle wheel. And then there was the *smell*. . . .

"What happened to my house?" Mrs. McGuire wailed.

Her husband gaped in horror. "We've been . . . trashed!"

Just then, Lanny and Matt appeared from behind one of the piles of twisted metal. Matt looked the sculpture up and down, and then placed a red wool sock on the front of it. Lanny's eyes were wide with awe.

"Finally, my work is complete," Matt said,

grinning with satisfaction. Lanny nodded, and they both turned to leave the room.

"Matt McGuire, what do you think you're doing?" Mrs. McGuire demanded.

"I call it *Ride Free from Golden Smog on Friday Afternoons,*" Matt said, as though the name made perfect sense.

Lanny gestured gracefully, clearly entranced with the magic of Matt's "art."

Mr. McGuire scowled. "I call it garbage."

"Garbage?" Matt looked horrified. "This is my passion."

"Oh, okay," Mrs. McGuire said. She really, really wanted to be supportive, but it was really, really hard when her living room looked like a junkyard. But she guessed that this was just the price she would have to pay for raising the next Picasso. "Well, if . . . if this is your passion, then we're here to encourage you, right, honey?"

Mr. McGuire nodded. "Even if it does smell."

Mrs. McGuire gave him a nudge with her elbow. Okay, so it smelled. It could have been worse. She wasn't sure how, but she knew that it could have been.

"Uh, keep up the good work, son," Mr. McGuire said halfheartedly. He guessed there was nothing to do now but put the groceries away. At least he wouldn't have to vacuum the living room rug anymore. He wouldn't want to suck up part of Matt's "art."

"So, what was it that you wanted to talk to me about?" Mrs. McGuire asked as she plopped down on Lizzie's bed later that evening.

That's right. i'm in over my head with all this Miranda stuff. i know when i need a professional, and i'm not afraid to admit it.

Lizzie sighed, and sat up. Her talk with Miranda that afternoon hadn't gotten her anywhere. If anything, things were worse now than they were before—now Miranda was mad at her, and she wasn't going to stop her diet, and she didn't even want to talk to Lizzie. *I can't believe my best friend picked a diet over me,* Lizzie thought miserably. *It just isn't like Miranda at all.* Lizzie felt like she had no choice—so she had to turn to the one person she thought might have some answers—her mom. "I have this friend . . ." Lizzie started.

The corner of Mrs. McGuire's mouth twitched up into a smile. "A friend, huh?" she asked knowingly, propping herself up on one arm.

"Yeah," Lizzie agreed. "And all of a sudden, she's become all . . ." Lizzie shook her head, groping for the right words. "Body conscious."

"Body conscious?" Mrs. McGuire repeated. She sat up quickly, frowning with concern. "What do you mean?"

"You know—" Lizzie prompted. "Like, she thinks she's fat—"

"Lizzie, that's ridiculous, honey!" her mom insisted. "You're not fat, you're perfect!"

"Mom," Lizzie said impatiently. "I'm talking about a friend here, remember?"

"Okay," Mrs. McGuire said dubiously. "Right."

Lizzie shook her head, flustered. Did her mom seriously think that Lizzie had an eating problem? Like, hadn't she noticed the plate and a half of spaghetti Lizzie had just downed for dinner?

"And it just doesn't make any sense that she's going on a diet," Lizzie continued earnestly, "because Miranda *so* is not fat—"

"Miranda?" Mrs. McGuire cried. "Is she

okay? Wait a minute. This doesn't have anything to do with what happened here the other day, does it? Honey, what kind of diet is she on?" Mrs. McGuire's voice was bordering on hysterical. "It's not one of those scary, trendy diets—"

Sheez, what do you do when your *professional* starts to freak out?

"Mom, Mom, Mom!" Lizzie held out her hands in an attempt to calm her mother down. She had enough things to worry about without her mom going completely ballistic. "Please," she begged. "I just . . . I don't know what I can do to help her."

Mrs. McGuire took a deep breath. "Well,"

she said slowly, "have you tried talking to her?"

Lizzie nodded. "She got mad at me."

"Well." Mrs. McGuire took Lizzie's hand. "If things don't change in a few days, why don't I sit down with Miranda and her mother. You know, to talk about it."

Lizzie swallowed hard. Just when she was beginning to think that this approach may have been a big mistake, her mom managed to come through. "That sounds good."

Mrs. McGuire nodded. "Good."

Lizzie sighed. "Thanks, Mom," she whispered.

Mom can be really smart sometimes. i'm glad i take after her.

Mrs. McGuire pulled her daughter close and hugged her, and, for the first time during this whole thing, Lizzie really believed that somehow things were going to be okay. They had to be.

CHAPTER SIX

"How bad was the fight you guys got into, anyway?" Gordo asked as he adjusted the special lighting he had set up in the school hallway.

Lizzie shook her head. She was dressed and ready for the video. But Miranda hadn't shown up yet, and the truth was, Lizzie wasn't sure that she would.

Just then, Miranda walked through the door. She was wearing a white satin shirt, and her hair was perfectly styled. She was clearly ready for the video shoot.

Lizzie grinned. "Miranda," she said happily. "You made it."

Miranda didn't smile back. "I said I'd be here," she said defensively.

"Look, Lizzie filled me in on what happened," Gordo said quickly, "and I'm really sorry if what I said freaked you out. You know, the food comment. I totally didn't mean it." He looked incredibly guilty, as though this entire mess was his fault.

"Whatever, Gordo," Miranda snapped. She looked down at the faux fur bag that was slung over her shoulder. "Are we going to shoot this?"

Lizzie looked over at Gordo, who glanced back miserably. Lizzie knew that she had to say something—she just couldn't let Miranda stay this angry forever. "Miranda, wait,"

Lizzie said. "Look, I'm really sorry about what happened at the mall. You're right, it's your body, it's your life, and it's your business." She pressed her lips together and forced herself to go on. The truth was, she didn't want to let this go. She cared about Miranda too much to sit back while she was hurting herself. "But I guess I just said that stuff because I really care about you and . . . you're scaring me."

Miranda blinked in surprise. She swallowed hard. "I am?" she asked in a small voice.

"You're scaring the both of us," Gordo admitted. "What's going on?"

Miranda sighed, and her body seemed to relax. "I don't know," she admitted. Miranda sat down on the steps and shook her head. "It's, like, all of a sudden, everything just feels out of control." Tears started to well up in her eyes. "My homework's piling up; my parents are talking to me about my 'future.' Things that used to feel so easy just now seem so hard."

"Well, call me blond," Lizzie said gently, "but what does all that have to do with losing weight?"

Miranda thought for a moment. "I guess eating is the only thing I have any control over," she said finally. "Like all this other stuff just happens to me, but eating's something I have a say in."

Gordo looked down at her sympathetically. "That's not true."

"That's how it feels." The tears in Miranda's eyes threatened to spill over.

"Miranda," Lizzie said, "that's why you have us. I mean, all this stuff that you're talking about, all this pressure, I'm going through it, too."

"Ditto," Gordo agreed.

Lizzie swallowed hard to clear the lump in her throat. "But what really helps me deal is you guys," she said. "And I know that no matter what, you and Gordo are always going to be there for me."

Miranda nodded. Her chin was quivering. "But doesn't it ever feel like sometimes it's all just too much?" she asked.

"Try every day," Lizzie admitted.

"But that's what we have each other for," Gordo added.

"I mean, no matter what, we're always going to be there for you," Lizzie said. And she meant it.

A tear welled up and trickled down the side of Miranda's nose. "I just don't know what to say."

"Well," Lizzie said slowly, "did you eat breakfast?"

Miranda gave a half-laugh, then a sniff. "No," she admitted.

"Well, that's good," Gordo told her, "because breakfast is in our budget." He jerked his head in the direction of the exit. "Let's go."

"You guys," Miranda said quietly. "Thanks."

Lizzie smiled. At last, they had gotten to the part where Miranda said thank you.

"Mom and Dad," Matt said as he led his parents outside. "Since you've been so supportive of my art, I've decided to break my own rule and let you observe me at work."

Mrs. McGuire nodded eagerly. "Oh!"

"What an honor," Mr. McGuire added.

"Where is it, honey?" Mrs. McGuire asked.

Matt waved his arm, and his parents turned to see. Lanny stood grinning beside the McGuires' station wagon, which looked like it had just escaped from an explosion in a paint factory. A riot of color was splattered over the side . . . no, over the *entire* car. For a moment, Mr. McGuire wasn't sure that he was seeing correctly. Then he realized the awful truth—he was seeing just fine. This was Matt's latest "art project."

"That's my car!" Mr. McGuire wailed.

Matt nodded in satisfaction. "I think it's my masterpiece."

"You turned your father's car into a masterpiece?" Mrs. McGuire cried.

"But that's my car!" Mr. McGuire wailed again.

Matt shook his head as he regarded the brilliantly hued station wagon. "My teacher's right," Matt said. "I have a gift."

Mr. McGuire looked at his wife. Then he took a deep breath. "Here's the deal, Matt," he said reasonably. Then he broke into his wail again. "That's my car!"

"From now on, I think you better stick to paper and paint," Mrs. McGuire said to her son. "In a room. With a smock."

Lanny covered his mouth with his hand and shook his head in dismay.

Mrs. McGuire patted Matt gently on the arm, so that he would know that she wasn't punishing him. Then again, she did have to rein him in before he got completely out of control. What was next—painting all the windows on the house magenta and puce? Sticking wire antennae on the neighbors' dog's head?

"What?" Matt cried, outraged. "I can't contain myself to a mere piece of paper!" he insisted. "Where's the challenge?"

"That *is* the challenge," Mr. McGuire pointed out. "You know, containing yourself. Like I am right now." Mr. McGuire gritted his teeth, his jaw muscles working furiously.

Mrs. McGuire looked at the car again. The new paint certainly made the station wagon unique. And there was something else that was different. . . . "Sam?" she asked, realizing what the change she noticed was.

"What?" Mr. McGuire growled.

"You can't see the dent where you hit the mailbox anymore," Mrs. McGuire pointed out.

"That's what Lanny said," Matt agreed.

Lanny nodded enthusiastically.

Mr. McGuire peered at the front fender, where brilliant flames, like the rays of the sun, curled outward. The dent *was* hidden by one of the flame's tongues, but Mr. McGuire was about to explode—and there was no hiding *that*!

* * *

Lizzie and Miranda sat on the floor as Gordo popped the tape into the VCR. Then he pressed PLAY and came to sit with them. Miranda reached into a bowl of popcorn as the video started to play.

On-screen, Lizzie and Miranda sat in detention. A stern-looking teacher—played by their English teacher's friend, Anthony—scowled at them. Anthony was a professional dancer, and a pretty good actor, too. And, best of all, he had agreed to be in Gordo's video for free.

In the scene, Miranda looked at Lizzie, and then pulled out a tiny radio. Miranda cranked up the volume, and the music kicked in.

Suddenly, Lizzie and Miranda skipped out of their chairs and pulled off their conservative sweaters, revealing satin shirts underneath. Miranda brushed the papers from the stern teacher's desk, and she and Lizzie stood on top of it. They hit a few dance moves, then jumped down and spun him around in his desk chair. Miranda grabbed an apple from his desk and shoved it in his mouth, then Lizzie and Miranda rolled him out the door and down the hall.

Out in the hallway, Lizzie and Miranda hit their dance moves. They were smooth like Janet and quick like Christina as they spun each other down the hall. Then Lizzie hurtled into a few flip-flops and midair somersaults— moves she remembered from her grade-school gym classes—and Miranda showed off a couple of hot moves, too.

Then Anthony ditched his stern-teacher persona and busted a few moves himself. It was great!

The music built to a climax, then cut off. Miranda and Lizzie hit their final poses, grinning.

"Wow, Gordo!" Lizzie gushed as Gordo stopped the tape. "That was so awesome. I didn't know you could make such a good vidco!"

Gordo smiled at her.

"Ohmigosh," Miranda said, staring at the television screen. "Look at me."

Lizzie put a reassuring hand on Miranda's arm. "You look fine, Miranda."

"Really, Miranda," Gordo chimed in, "you look totally fine."

"Fine?" Miranda demanded, scowling at Lizzie. "I look—I look amazing! Did you see me?" Miranda grinned broadly.

Lizzie looked at Gordo. "Yeah," she said, smiling. "You looked good."

"No, no, no, *you* look *good*," Miranda corrected her friend, "but did you see *me*?"

Gordo elbowed Miranda in the ribs. "Miranda, come on."

"Seriously," Miranda said, wide-eyed. "Can we watch it again? Can I get copies?" She grabbed the remote from Gordo's hand.

"Miranda . . ." Lizzie said, smiling.

But there was nothing else to say. Her best friend was back.

With a vengeance.

PART TWO

CHAPTER ONE

Lizzie dribbled the basketball and heaved it to Gordo, who bounced it between his legs, faking out Ethan Craft just as Lizzie ducked past Miranda. A moment later, Gordo hit a basket from downtown. Boo-yah! Three points for Gordo and Lizzie, the dynamic duo.

"Nice one, Gordo!" Lizzie shouted, as Gordo pumped his fist into the air.

"This is Gordo's house!" Gordo sounded like he was in a Nike commercial.

Lizzie rolled her eyes. "Who talks like that?" she demanded, planting her hands on her hips.

"Gimme the rock," Ethan said, holding out his hands for the basketball.

Miranda looked at Lizzie. "Ethan does."

So—okay, apparently this court-speak was a male phenomenon. Of course, Ethan Craft was so hot that you could practically fry an egg on his forehead, so he could be excused for the inane chatter. Let's face it, Lizzie thought as she stared at Ethan's gleaming hair, everything works for Ethan.

Miranda grabbed the ball at half-court. She faked a shot and then passed the ball quickly to Ethan. But Lizzie and Gordo had Ethan double-teamed, so he shot a pass back to his partner, Miranda, who had been left open while Lizzie and Gordo guarded Ethan.

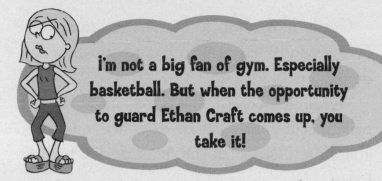

i'm not a big fan of gym. Especially basketball. But when the opportunity to guard Ethan Craft comes up, you take it!

"Oh, Miranda's got game!" Miranda cried excitedly as she dribbled the basketball.

Lizzie pouted. She was not making a good impression on Ethan, and *that* had to change. "I want game!" she griped as Miranda lobbed the ball. *Swish*—all net!

"Our game was busy guarding Ethan," Gordo said, giving Lizzie his patented eye-rolling thing.

True. But it was worth every second.

Gordo looked up to check the time clock. Five seconds left. "Watch and see how it's done," he told Lizzie.

Gordo grabbed the basketball and took the ball to half-court. Ethan extended his arms, guarding Gordo, so he passed the ball to Lizzie.

The timer ticked down. Miranda was guarding Lizzie pretty aggressively—Lizzie didn't have a shot. She tossed a bounce-pass back to Gordo. He faked a pass to Lizzie, and Ethan fell for it. The minute Ethan lunged toward the fake pass, Gordo drove hard in the opposite direction. He spun around Ethan and blazed toward the basket.

Only two seconds left! Gordo went for the jump shot. It's going to go in! Lizzie thought, pumping her fist in the air. Lizzie and Gordo would never win, but at least they'd have made a classic shot before the game ended!

But just then, Ethan swooped in behind Gordo and swatted the ball. Rejected! With one second left, the ball flew into the next zip code.

The buzzer let out an ear-piercing squeal. Game over. The score was 24–8.

Gordo stared at the hoop, as though he still couldn't believe that the ball hadn't gone in. His jaw hung slack.

Lizzie walked up behind him and patted him on the back. "Is that how it's done, Gordo?" she joked gently.

"How did he do that?" Gordo asked.

"Maybe next time, little man," Ethan said to Gordo. He picked up the ball and gave it a bounce, as Miranda congratulated him on their awesome win.

Lizzie watched Ethan walk away. "Is there anything Ethan can't do?" she asked with a sigh.

"Yeah," Gordo said bitterly, "count past ten without taking his shoes off."

But if he was cute and smart, he'd be Super Ethan. And i don't think the universe is ready for that. But i am!

Lizzie glared at her best friend and folded her arms across her chest. Did Gordo really have to point out all of Ethan's flaws? So what if Ethan wasn't Einstein? The world needed hotness as much as it needed that math junk. In fact, Lizzie thought, maybe the world needed hotness more—it was so much easier to understand.

"Can we talk about something else?" Gordo snapped.

"How about who Ethan's going to ask to the dance Friday?" Lizzie suggested, grinning brightly. She had a few ideas about who might make the perfect date. . . .

Miranda nodded, grinning eagerly. They were both into Ethan, and his utter gorgeousness.

Me! Me! Me! Me! Me! Me! i mean, i don't care. Whatever.

Gordo's eyebrows disappeared beneath his curly mop of hair as he flashed Miranda and Lizzie a dubious look. He pointed to his best friends. "I doubt he's going to ask you guys."

"Gordo!" Lizzie and Miranda wailed in unison.

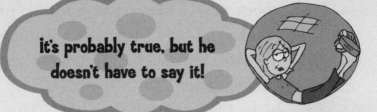
it's probably true, but he doesn't have to say it!

"You're just saying that 'cause *you* don't have a date for the dance," Miranda told Gordo defensively.

Gordo sighed. "Look, middle school is hard enough without the added pressure of who I'm taking to the dance."

"So I guess we're all three going together?" Lizzie suggested. "Cool."

Gordo shrugged. He didn't look too excited about the idea, but Lizzie was. Hey— if she couldn't have Ethan, the next best thing was being at the dance with her best friends.

"I guess we're just the three amigos flying solo," Miranda said happily.

Lizzie giggled. Going stag was so much

easier when you had friends like Gordo and Miranda around.

Just then, Parker McKenzie walked up to them. She was still wearing her gym uniform, but she didn't look like she'd just spent the past forty-five minutes playing basketball. Why am I the only one who seems to work up a sweat in this class? Lizzie wondered.

"Hey, guys," Parker chirped.

"Hey, Parker," Lizzie and Miranda said.

"Hey." Gordo gave Parker a little wave.

"So, Gordo," Parker said. "You're a pretty good basketball player."

Lizzie had to stifle a laugh. Was Parker kidding? Gordo was the worst basketball player in the eighth grade! He was even worse than Lizzie! At least *she* managed to pass the ball— even if it was to people on the other team.

Gordo looked confused. "I am?" he asked. Then he seemed to realize what he was saying, and covered quickly. "Oh, yeah, I am," he agreed, grinning confidently.

Parker complimenting Gordo on basketball? You don't think . . .? Nah!

"Yeah," Parker went on, "you were totally robbed of that last basket." She flipped her long, straight brown hair over her shoulder.

"Thanks," Gordo said, nodding. "I was."

Parker looked up at the clock, then looked back at Gordo and smiled. "See you around." Then she turned to Miranda and Lizzie, as though she had only just then even realized they were standing there. "Later," she said to them.

Gordo smiled as he watched Parker walk away.

Lizzie cocked an eyebrow. "What was *that*?" she demanded, laughing a little.

Gordo made an expression that clearly said, I Have No Idea.

"Apparently, *that* was Gordo's new best friend, Parker," Miranda said.

"I think I'm going to ask her to the dance," Gordo said absently, still watching Parker.

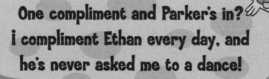

One compliment and Parker's in? I compliment Ethan every day, and he's never asked me to a dance!

"But what about our no-dates-to-the-dance policy?" Lizzie asked. Suddenly, Gordo was flushing the whole idea of going solo-with-amigos—without even consulting her and Miranda? That didn't seem fair.

"What, I can change my mind," Gordo said reasonably. "Maybe it's time to take a chance. Live a little." Gordo rubbed his hands together and walked off. Lizzie and Miranda stared after him.

"Well, I guess it's just the two amigos," Miranda noted.

"Yeah, well," Lizzie folded her arms across her chest, "you're a better dancer than Gordo, anyway."

That was pretty much the understatement of the century, Lizzie thought as she watched Gordo's retreating figure. Still, for some reason, she couldn't help feeling kind of disappointed.

CHAPTER TWO

"Hey, Matt," Mr. McGuire said as his son walked into the kitchen and dropped his book bag down beside the kitchen island. Mr. and Mrs. McGuire were in the middle of preparing dinner. Mr. McGuire was peeling potatoes, and Mrs. McGuire was chopping up vegetables for a salad.

"How was your day?" Mrs. McGuire asked.

"I need to talk to you guys," Matt said. His voice was serious.

Mr. and Mrs. McGuire looked at each

other. Usually, when Matt needed to talk to them, it did not mean good news was on its way.

"One day," Mrs. McGuire begged, "could we have one day without him getting into trouble?"

Mr. McGuire cleared his throat and braced himself. "What's up?"

"We have to kind of give a report at school about our ancestors," Matt admitted. "And I was wondering"—Matt looked at them hopefully—"do we have any ancestors?"

Mr. and Mrs. McGuire looked at each other and sighed with relief.

"Of course we do," Mr. McGuire said. "What kind of stuff do you need to know?"

Matt shrugged. "Not much—just where we came from and stuff."

"Oh, well, my grandparents came here from Poland during World War Two," Mrs. McGuire volunteered. "My grandfather worked on an assembly line in a candy factory, and my grandmother worked in a hospital, making beds." She smiled at Matt, as though this was terrific material for a world-class report.

Matt nodded. "Interesting." Then he turned to his father. "Please, tell me you've got something better than that," he said desperately. "Please!"

Mr. McGuire lifted his eyebrows. "How about William 'Braveheart' Wallace?" he asked proudly. "The guy who freed Scotland from English rule."

Matt grinned eagerly. "That's pretty good."

Mrs. McGuire gave her husband a look. "If it was true. Which it's not," she said, turning back to face Matt. "Your father came from dairy farmers in Kalamazoo."

"I'm just trying to spice it up a little," Mr. McGuire offered.

"He doesn't need spice," Mrs. McGuire snapped. "He needs to know about his family history."

"I was just hoping that we were related to someone famous," Matt admitted. "I mean, Lanny is related to Crispus Attucks. He was the first American to be killed in the Revolutionary War."

"Really?" Mr. McGuire said, putting down his potato peeler. "That's pretty cool."

Matt heaved a disappointed sigh. "But I guess we're just the boring McGuires. I'll just go upstairs and write my boring report." Matt slung his book bag over his shoulder and headed to his room, dreading the assignment. "Dairy farmers," he muttered, shaking his head. This was going to be even more boring than he had feared, if *that* were possible.

Later that afternoon, Lizzie, Gordo, and

Miranda hooked up at their favorite cyber-café, the Digital Bean.

"So," Lizzie asked Gordo, "did you ask her yet?" Lizzie nodded toward Parker, who was sitting alone at a nearby table, doing homework.

"Uh, no," Gordo admitted. He, Lizzie, and Miranda were seated on the plush couches in the corner of the café. Gordo was keeping his back toward Parker in an effort to look casual.

"So, what?" Lizzie asked. "You changed your mind?"

"Well," Gordo hedged. "No."

Lizzie had never seen her best friend look so uncomfortable.

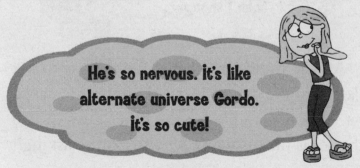

He's so nervous. It's like alternate universe Gordo. It's so cute!

"Well," Lizzie urged, "go ask her."

"Yeah," Miranda agreed, rolling her eyes. "It's not that hard."

"Have you ever asked Ethan Craft out to a dance, Miranda?" Gordo asked his friend.

"No!" Miranda replied.

"And why not?" Gordo demanded.

Miranda sighed. Okay, so Gordo had a point. "Because it would be so embarrassing," she admitted. "Mortifying."

"Exactly." Gordo shrugged.

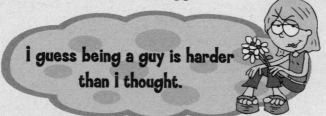

i guess being a guy is harder than i thought.

All the more reason that Gordo has to ask Parker to the dance, Lizzie thought. He has to set a good example for the other guys . . . so that girls like us won't *have* to do the asking!

"Come on, Gordo," Lizzie urged gently, gesturing in Parker's direction. "You can do this."

"Yeah," Miranda agreed. "The worst she can say is, uh . . ."—Miranda nodded her head and smiled—"no."

"But if she did, then you'd just be stuck with us," Lizzie said quickly. "But she won't," Lizzie added, giggling nervously.

Gordo heaved a deep breath. "Okay," he said finally, throwing up his hands in defeat, "wish me luck." He hauled himself off the couch and made his way over to Parker's table.

Gor-do! Gor-do! Gor-do!
Gor-do! Gor-do! Gor-do!

Lizzie gestured to Miranda, and the two girls hopped off the couch and tiptoed over to a nearby booth, where they crouched behind the high back of the seat. An older guy who was sitting in the booth, drinking a latte, gave them a weird look and hurried away. Whatever. All the better to overhear Gordo's conversation, Lizzie thought. Not that she was eavesdropping. But . . . if she happened to overhear what happened, that wouldn't really be her fault, would it?

Gordo slid into the seat across from Parker, who looked up and smiled. "Hey, Parker," Gordo said.

"Hey."

"So, um . . ." Gordo looked around, obviously trying to find something to say. Finally, his eyes settled on the open book in front of Parker. "Math homework, huh?"

Parker nodded. "Yeah."

"Yeah," Gordo said nodding. "Lots of math homework."

"Yeah, it is," Parker agreed. She twirled the pencil in her hand.

"So," Gordo said suddenly, shifting uncomfortably in his chair. "Did you hear the one about the king of Norway?"

Meanwhile, Miranda was hiding behind a large gold tassel that hung from the high back of the booth, so she didn't have a very good view of what was happening. "So, what's going on?" she whispered to Lizzie.

Lizzie grimaced. She couldn't exactly hear what Gordo and Parker were saying, so she was trying to figure out their body language. But even that was kind of vague . . . and she was starting to get worried. "It doesn't look good," she said.

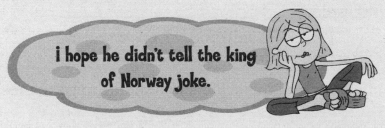

i hope he didn't tell the king of Norway joke.

"Oh," Lizzie said suddenly, "I think he's gonna ask . . ." Her stomach fluttered with about a thousand queasy butterflies.

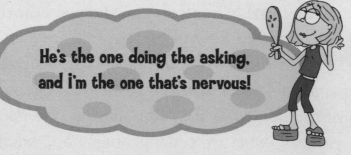

He's the one doing the asking, and i'm the one that's nervous!

"Well, it was great talking to you, Gordo," Parker said as she slid her books into her book bag, "but I've got to motor."

Gordo nodded. "Oh, okay."

Lizzie watched as Gordo and Parker stood up. It was weird—Lizzie had never noticed before, but Parker was slightly taller than Gordo.

"Parker," Gordo said, "I was wondering . . ."

Parker nodded eagerly. "Uh-huh?"

"Do you think you'd maybe like to go to the

dance with me?" Gordo smiled awkwardly.

Lizzie's heart lurched. This was it. He was asking. . . .

"Oh. Wow," Parker said. "Um, I'm sorry," she said, wincing. "I can't."

Gordo rubbed his hands together, and stared down at the table as Parker gave him a weak smile, then walked away.

"Looks like a no," Lizzie whispered to Miranda, who nodded.

Gordo stood there without moving, looking like someone had just stepped on his best video camera. It was most definitely a no.

"Maybe I'm related to Mark McGwire?" Matt said hopefully, thinking about the all-star baseball slugger as he tapped away at the computer keyboard in the living room.

Lanny chuckled, silently of course, but then he caught himself.

"It could happen," Matt said defensively. He grabbed the mouse and clicked SEARCH.

Lanny stared at the computer monitor, shaking his head.

Matt glared at his friend. "I can't believe you're related to Crispus Attucks," he said enviously. "I mean, he's an American patriot—"

Lanny put his hand over his heart.

Matt could just picture Lanny's report. It would be full of exciting details about his ancestors' bravery and patriotism. Lanny was so lucky! "And I have to follow it up with a report that says I'm related to Kalamazoo dairy farmers," Matt said miserably. His own report would be full of nonexciting details about cows and cheese and stuff.

Lanny shrugged and started to gather his books.

"Okay," Matt said with a sigh. "I guess I'll see you tomorrow, Lanny."

Lanny waved and turned to go. Matt faced the computer monitor. He clicked the mouse a couple of times and scanned the screen, hoping to find something—anything—interesting to put in his report.

"This is hard," Matt complained. "I mean, there's so much out there. I could be related to George Washington and not even know it." Matt's eyes lit up. He'd suddenly had an idea—a *brilliant* idea! "And no one else would know it, either!"

Sure—now that Matt thought about it, he realized that he kind of looked like George Washington. Without the wooden teeth and powdered wig, of course.

"Or maybe I could remember the Alamo!" Matt added. Of course, Matt and Davy Crockett had a lot in common. Like they both . . . well . . . were human beings.

"Or maybe . . . Elvis," Matt improvised.

"Yeah, that's it. Vegas, baby," he said in his best Elvis Presley voice. "Vegas."

Matt started typing like crazy. This report was starting to get interesting.

Lizzie stirred her smoothie as Gordo plopped onto the stool beside her at the Digital Bean's counter. "Okay," Lizzie said, "so tell me exactly what Parker said."

"She said, 'Sorry, I can't.'" Gordo shook his head.

"But it looked like everything was going great," Lizzie protested. Parker had seemed happy to see Gordo when he walked over to her table. And I mean, Parker actually complimented Gordo on his basketball skills! Lizzie thought. Either the girl is crazy about him, or else she's just plain *crazy*.

"Yeah, I know," Gordo admitted. "I, I guess I'm just the guy you say 'hi' to in the hallway, but not the guy you actually go out with."

"No, Gordo." Lizzie bit her lip. She had the definite feeling that something weird was going on. "That doesn't make sense."

"It's Parker," Miranda said, making a sour face. "She's weird." Miranda took a sip of her smoothie.

Lizzie glanced over toward the front door. Parker was standing nearby, chatting with a friend. She hadn't left yet.

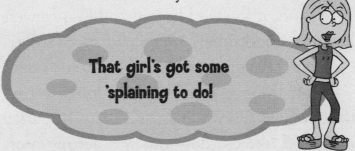

That girl's got some 'splaining to do!

"I'm going to be right back," Lizzie said as she slid down from her stool and hurried toward where Parker was standing.

Parker had just finished talking to her

friend and was turning to leave as Lizzie caught up to her. "Uh, Parker," Lizzie called.

"Oh, hi, Lizzie," Parker said, hugging her books against her chest.

"Hey," Lizzie gave Parker a little smile. The truth was, Lizzie had never been wild about Parker. But she felt like she owed it to Gordo to find out what the deal was. After all, she had talked him into asking out Parker in the first place.

"So, uh, it looked like you and Gordo were having a good time," Lizzie said awkwardly.

"Yeah," Parker admitted. "He's pretty cool."

"Yeah, he is," Lizzie agreed, looking over her shoulder at Gordo again. Okay, so Parker really did like Gordo—this was getting more bizarre by the second. Lizzie turned back to Parker. "So, why did you turn him down for the dance?"

"Because he's short," Parker whispered.

That's not a reason! I can't go because my cat died is a reason!

Lizzie let out an exasperated sigh. "Parker," she said, trying to be patient, "*you* are short."

"Listen, Lizzie, I know he's your friend—" Parker said. "He's a great guy to hang out with and all—but I don't want to go out with a short guy. Later." Parker turned on her heel and walked out the door.

Furious, Lizzie turned back toward Miranda and Gordo. But one look at Gordo's face made Lizzie's anger evaporate into shock. He had obviously overheard the whole thing. I'm such an idiot, Lizzie thought miserably. Why didn't I pull Parker into the girls' room to talk to her?

"Parker is such a witch!" Miranda snarled.

It's a good thing Gordo doesn't care what other people think.

But Gordo's face . . . Lizzie had never seen him look so hurt.

Or maybe not.

"Are you okay, Gordo?" Lizzie asked gently.

"Yeah," Gordo said quickly. "Never been better." Then he hurried out of the Digital Bean without saying good-bye.

Miranda stared after him. "Lizzie, what just happened?" she asked.

Lizzie shook her head. "I don't know."

CHAPTER THREE

"**S**o, have you talked to Gordo since yesterday?" Miranda asked. She and Lizzie were seated at their table on the lunch patio. Gordo was usually the first one there . . . but now it was ten minutes into lunch, and he still hadn't shown. Not a good sign.

Lizzie sighed. "I tried calling him, but his parents said he was doing homework."

Miranda brightened. "He was doing homework?" she asked. "See, I told you he'd get over it."

"I don't know," Lizzie said as she stared down at the slice of pizza on her tray. "I've never seen Gordo take anything so personally. I mean, it's Gordo." Gordo was always giving Lizzie and Miranda lectures about "being their own person" and "not following the herd." He had always been the one who didn't pay attention to what anyone thought. . . .

But now, I guess he's paying attention, Lizzie thought miserably.

"Yeah. I know," Miranda agreed. "He's usually the one telling us not to care what other people think."

it's like we've switched identities.

Just then, Gordo walked out onto the lunch patio. For a moment, Lizzie was so happy to see him that she didn't even notice that there was something different about him. Then he stumbled, and Lizzie realized that Gordo was actually wearing cowboy boots. Definitely a bizarre fashion statement, Lizzie thought—even for him. Still, she didn't want to seem down on the boots. Gordo needed all of the encouragement he could get.

"Nice boots," Lizzie said.

Miranda was blunter. "What are you doing? Running away to a rodeo or something?"

Gordo picked up a boot. They had pretty thick heels, and probably added a good few inches to his height. "What, these?" he asked quickly. "I've had them forever. I've worn 'em, like, a million times."

Hold it right there, pardner. i don't think you're telling the truth.

Gordo slid into the seat across from Lizzie.

Miranda was still staring at his boots. "The price tag is still on them."

Gordo ignored her.

"Gordo, about yesterday—" Lizzie began.

"I'm fine," Gordo said, waving his hand dismissively. "Did you know that the average fourteen-year-old male is five foot six? Which makes me only four inches shorter than the average fourteen-year-old male."

Lizzie rolled her eyes, wondering if he was four inches shorter with or without those lame boots on. "Well, good for the average fourteen-year-old male, then. But, Gordo, you've always been above average."

"Exactly," Gordo agreed. "And most males hit their growth spurt by fifteen. Which means I still have a year to grow. Everything's cool." Gordo grinned.

"So, you're cool with Ethan and Parker going to the dance together," Miranda put in.

Gordo's smile disappeared.

Lizzie glared at Miranda. Usually, Lizzie loved her best friend's Tell-It-Like-It-Is style, but right now, she was wishing that Miranda's attitude was more Sit-Quiet-and-Smile.

And the award for bad timing goes to . . .

Miranda's eyes widened as she realized what she had just done.

"Figures," Gordo said bitterly. "The tall guys get everything."

Lizzie scoffed. Gordo needed a serious reality check. "Since when is Parker 'everything'?"

With the way she treated Gordo, she's not anything.

"I know," Miranda agreed. "Ethan could do *so* much better."

Gordo glared at her, then turned to Lizzie and said, "That's not what I meant. . . ."

"What *did* you mean, then?" Lizzie asked.

"You guys are part of the problem, you know?" Gordo told her. "You buy into the whole tall-guy thing. Look at who you have a crush on—Ethan Craft."

Miranda touched her chest defensively. "We don't like him because he's tall."

"Why is it, then?" Gordo demanded, sneering. "Because he's smart?"

Miranda and Lizzie just looked at each

other. It was true—Ethan had the brains of a bread crumb.

"You know, just leave me alone. Forget it." Gordo stood up and stalked away from the table. . . . Well, he stalked as well as he could in his cowboy boots.

Miranda stared after him. "You know, I don't think I've ever seen Gordo this way."

What do you do when the person with all the answers is the person with the problem?

Gordo had helped Lizzie out a million times when she needed it. . . . She felt like she owed it to him to try to make this situation better. I'm going to help him whether he wants me to or not, Lizzie decided. "I'm gonna go talk to him."

"No," Miranda said firmly. "Just give him some time."

Lizzie looked at her friend. "What are we going to do?"

"He'll talk to us when he's ready," Miranda said.

And Lizzie just hoped that she was right.

CHAPTER FOUR

Lanny smiled as Mrs. Varga's class applauded. He'd just finished his oral presentation on Crispus Attucks, and it had blown everyone away. It would definitely be a tough act to follow.

"Well done, Lanny," Mrs. Varga said as Lanny took his seat. "Crispus Attucks—quite impressive. You must be quite proud to be related to an American patriot."

Lanny smiled at her and winked.

"And next up," Mrs. Varga went on, "we have Matt McGuire."

Matt got up and stood in front of the class. Then he pulled out the poster he had spent all night making. It was a timeline, going from the foundation of the McGuire clan—with George Washington—on to Davy Crockett, Elvis Presley, and right on up to Matt. Matt pulled out a powdered wig and tricornered hat. He thought the wig really showed off his resemblance to the first president of the United States.

"You know? We've all heard of George Washington as the founding father of this country," Matt began. "But who knew he was the founding father of my family?" Matt went on to talk about his lesser relatives who had lived over the years . . . the writer Ralph Waldo Emerson; Francis Scott Key, who wrote the national anthem. ". . . And then, the family moved to Texas, where they changed their name to Crockett," Matt went on. He took off his tricornered hat and wig, replacing them with a coonskin cap. "That's right," Matt said, "Davy Crockett, who made his last stand at the Alamo . . ."

A kid at the front of the class raised his hand. "But if Davy Crockett died at the Alamo, wouldn't that be the end of your family tree?"

"Please, hold your questions until the end," Matt said smoothly. "Thank you, and moving on . . ."

Matt went on to explain his family relationship to the Roosevelts—Teddy, Eleanor, and Franklin Delano—and the multimillionaire Rockefeller family. Finally, he came to the real highlight. He took off the coonskin cap and put on an Elvis wig and huge sunglasses. ". . . And then good ole Uncle Elvis picked up a guitar and changed the face of music forever." Matt grinned at the thought that he had been related to a bunch of presidents, and the one and only King. "That's right, I'm all shook up. From fighting for our country to fighting for rock and roll, the McGuires have not only seen history but they made it, baby. Thank you, thank you very much! Thank you." Matt struck an Elvis-style pose as the room exploded with applause.

Matt was so busy being adored that he didn't notice that one person wasn't clapping.

Lanny looked like he was about to give Matt a piece of his mind.

Gordo looked around. He was in class . . . but something was different. Everything looked bigger. It took a minute for Gordo to realize that everything else wasn't bigger—no, *he* was smaller. Somehow, he had shrunk down to a height of about six inches. He tried to use a rope to climb up on top of his desk, but it was no use. Besides—even if he made it up there—how would he take notes? The pen was as big as he was!

Later, Gordo found himself at a dance. He was standing beside a punch bowl, desperately trying to get a girl's attention, but his voice was so tiny that she couldn't even hear him. She finished her punch and put the cup down—almost crushing Gordo!

Once he had escaped from his near-death-by-punch-glass experience, Gordo made his way to the guidance counselor's office. She had just put up a new chart that read YOU MUST BE THIS TALL TO ATTEND HARVARD. Gordo went to stand beside it. He was nowhere near the cutoff.

Dejected, Gordo made his way home. He wanted to work on something fun for a change, so he tried to scramble into his director's chair. But it was no use. He was like a three-year-old trying to haul himself up into his dad's chair. He was just way too small!

Suddenly, the bell rang, and Gordo found himself facedown in his textbook. He sat up. For a moment, he was confused, and then he realized where he was . . . in class. He'd fallen asleep and had been dreaming. Disgusted, he picked up his books and walked out of the room. Time for gym, where he could get creamed by Ethan . . . as usual.

Gordo watched as Mr. Dig challenged Ethan Craft on the basketball court. Mr. Dig was the perennial substitute teacher at Hillridge Junior High—he seemed to be there every day, substituting for one class or another. This week, the hip young teacher was in for Coach Kelly in Physical Education. And he was definitely schooling Ethan. He ducked past

Ethan and made the shot over the tall guy's head. The buzzer rang—game over. Mr. Dig, who was a lot shorter than Ethan, had won by eight points.

"Nice game, Mr. Dig," Ethan congratulated the teacher, giving him a high five. "You got skills."

Mr. Dig grinned and shook his head. "Nah, you're just easy to beat," he replied.

"Come on, why you gotta be like that?" Ethan joked. Then he spotted Gordo, standing by the sidelines. "Hey, yo! Gor-don," Ethan called. He held out his hand for a high five, but Gordo ducked away.

"Hey," Gordo said, and he kept on walking toward Mr. Dig.

Ethan looked confused (even more so than usual) as Gordo walked away. Ethan and Gordo were usually pretty friendly, but now Ethan couldn't tell whether or not he had been dissed. He decided not to worry about it, though. He had figured out a long time ago that most confusing situations just worked themselves out if you ignored them long enough.

"Mr. Dig, how's a guy like you beat Ethan?" Gordo asked.

"Practice, Mr. Gordon, practice," Mr. Dig said confidently. "In fact, I taught Allen Iverson the crossover." With a deft movement, he whipped the ball in a neat semicircle. "There's no defense against it." Mr. Dig flashed Gordo a huge smile, but Gordo didn't respond. In fact, he hardly seemed to be paying attention to Mr. Dig at all—he was lost in thought. "This isn't about basketball, is it?" Mr. Dig realized.

"Not exactly," Gordo admitted.

Mr. Dig planted the basketball against his hip. "And so what's up?"

"Well, I asked Parker to the dance." Gordo frowned. "And she turned me down. The end."

Mr. Dig shrugged. "So a girl turned you down. When I was in middle school, I got turned down so many times, I thought I was a bedsheet." The substitute chuckled at his own joke and put his arm around Gordo's shoulders.

Gordo made a sour face. "She turned me down 'cause I'm short."

Mr. Dig's smile vanished. "Oh."

Gordo nodded. "Yeah." He pressed his lips together, then went on, "I guess I should be used to it by now, since I'm going to be like this for the rest of my life. My parents aren't exactly giants."

Mr. Dig sat down on the bench beside Gordo and leaned against the basketball in his lap. "You don't know how tall you're going to be. My parents are both over six feet tall. And I'm not exactly Shaquille O'Neal."

"I'm not any shorter today than I was last week." Gordo shook his head. This whole thing was just so embarrassing to talk about. His mind knew that this wasn't worth getting upset about, but his heart couldn't help it. Gordo didn't usually have problems like this. "It just never seemed to be so important before, and now it's all I can think about."

"Trust me, I get it," Mr. Dig said. "All I can tell you is that when I decided that being short didn't matter to me, it didn't matter to anyone else, either."

Gordo regarded Mr. Dig with a frank stare. "Well, it matters to Parker."

"Yeah, well, there'll be other Parkers," Mr. Dig promised. "But you don't want people like that in your life anyway."

"You know, Mr. Dig, you're not exactly making me feel better," Gordo said.

"I didn't say it to make you feel better," Mr. Dig replied. "I said it because it's the truth, Mr. Gordon." He patted Gordo on the back, then stood up. He darted gracefully toward the basket and made the easy layup.

Score two points for the short guy.

CHAPTER FIVE

Matt stormed into the kitchen, where his parents were busy restoring one of Mr. McGuire's old radio-controlled airplanes. "Lanny's not talking to me!" Matt confessed as he climbed onto a stool.

"How can he tell?" Mr. McGuire whispered to his wife.

Mrs. McGuire cleared her throat and turned to Matt, all sympathy. "What happened?"

"I faked my family history report—" Matt began.

"You *what?*" Mrs. McGuire cried.

"What did you *say?*" Mr. McGuire demanded. He couldn't believe that Matt hadn't talked about his family's proud dairy farming heritage.

"That we were related to George Washington, Davy Crockett, and Elvis," Matt admitted. He decided to leave out the others . . . they weren't that impressive, anyway.

Mrs. McGuire shook her head in amazement. Sometimes she was astounded by the incredibly complex and creative creature she had spawned. "What possessed you to do something like that?"

"Yeah," Mr. McGuire chimed in.

"I was jealous of Lanny," Matt admitted. "And Dad said it was okay to spice things up a little. . . ." he added quickly. For Matt, shifting blame was something of an art form.

Mrs. McGuire glared at her husband. "Nice job," she growled.

"The one time he listens to me!" Mr. McGuire threw up his hands in frustration.

"Matt, you can't *choose* who you're related to," Mrs. McGuire said patiently. "You have to be proud of where you come from."

Matt looked at the floor. "I only wish I had known that a couple of hours ago."

"Well, you can change your future," Mr. McGuire suggested. "You can start by apologizing to Lanny."

"That's a great idea, Dad," Matt said. His dad was right—he had to phone Lanny right away. "I hope Lanny'll still talk to me," he murmured as he scurried out of the kitchen.

Mr. McGuire pumped his fists in the air. "Great parenting comeback by Sam McGuire! Woo-hoo! Woo-hoo!"

Mrs. McGuire looked at him. "You do realize that we forgot to punish him for lying on his report?"

Mr. McGuire did his best to ignore her. "Can't I just have *one* moment?"

Lizzie regarded herself in the mirror, then added a little lip gloss. She wished that she was more excited about the dance, but it just didn't seem like fun now that Gordo wasn't going. Part of her wanted to call Miranda and cancel, but another part of her was still holding out hope that maybe Gordo would show after all, and that they could be the three solo amigos, just like they had planned.

Right, like that will happen, Lizzie told herself.

Just then, there was a gentle knock at the door, and Mrs. McGuire poked her head into Lizzie's room. "Honey, you have a visitor." Mrs.

McGuire stepped aside, and Gordo walked into the room. He was wearing a button-down shirt and a jacket—dance clothes.

"Hey," Gordo said quietly.

"Gordo?" Lizzie turned away from her mirror to face him.

Gordo walked over to her desk chair and sat down. "I owe you an apology."

"For what?"

"'Cause I said you were part of the problem, when I've got the problem," Gordo admitted.

Lizzie sighed. "Gordo, I had no idea that it bothered you so much."

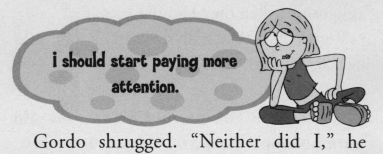

i should start paying more attention.

Gordo shrugged. "Neither did I," he

admitted. "But it just really hurt, you know? I've always been told that I can do whatever I want."

"Because you can," Lizzie said earnestly. She really meant it. If there was one person in the world who could do whatever he wanted, that person was Gordo.

Gordo winced. "No, I can't. I can't make myself grow."

"Why would you want to?" Lizzie asked gently. "To make everyone else happy?"

"Look," Gordo said. "I know that I tell you and Miranda all the time that who you are as a person is more important than how you look. But this one's tough, Lizzie. This one I can't control." He glanced at Lizzie, then had to look away. "I don't know, I guess I'm a hypocrite."

"No, you're not a hypocrite," Lizzie said warmly. "You're normal."

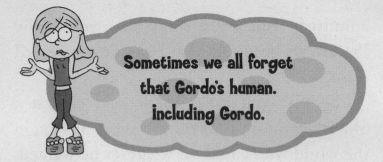

Sometimes we all forget
that Gordo's human.
including Gordo.

"Miranda and I like you just the way you are," Lizzie went on, wishing that she had the words to tell Gordo how special he was. No matter how short or tall he was, he would always be her best friend. Because he would always be Gordo.

"I like who I am, too," Gordo admitted. "I would just like to be taller."

"Hey, I like who I am, but I'd like to be Britney Spears," Lizzie said brightly. "But it's not going to happen."

Gordo smiled at her. "I guess it's kind of silly when you put it that way."

Lizzie nodded and said, "Yeah, it is."

We've made contact!
Gordo is in the building!

"I mean, Gordo, you're smart and you're funny and . . ." How can I put this? Lizzie thought. "A little weird sometimes," she admitted.

Gordo laughed.

"But I wouldn't like you any other way," Lizzie finished.

"Thanks," Gordo smiled and stood up. Lizzie stood up, too, and Gordo gave her a big hug.

"So," Gordo said as he pulled away. "You, uh, wanna go to the dance with me?"

Lizzie grinned. "Actually, you know, I don't really date guys with . . . uh . . ." She wracked her brain to come up with something that would make Gordo laugh. "Blue eyes."

"I see." Gordo nodded seriously. Then he picked up a fuzzy blue pillow and whacked Lizzie on the shoulder with it, and they both burst into giggles.

"But I guess just this once I'll make a little exception," Lizzie said, smiling. Then she grabbed the pillow and whacked him back.

CHAPTER SIX

Gordo and Lizzie walked into the gym, which was decorated for the dance with streamers and colored lights. Loud music blared from speakers nearby. Most of the kids were already out on the dance floor, but Miranda had staked out the refreshments table.

"Gordo," Miranda cried as her friends joined her by the punch bowl. "You, you made it!" Her eyes dropped to Gordo's feet. "And no cowboy boots?"

Gordo gave her a wry smile. "Yeah, they weren't exactly me."

Miranda nodded knowingly. "Good choice."

"Um, hello?" Lizzie said. Miranda hadn't even glanced in her direction yet.

"Oh, I'm sorry, Lizzie, I was talking to my date," Miranda joked.

"Actually," Lizzie said, putting her hand on Gordo's shoulder, "he's my date!"

Gordo smiled at his friends. "Thanks."

Miranda grinned and nodded toward the dance floor. "Check out Ethan. Parker looks like she's having a *great* time," she said, her voice dripping with sarcasm.

Lizzie followed Miranda's gaze over to where Ethan was busting a move. That is, he was busting *something*. He was dancing wildly, almost like he was on the receiving end of some serious electric shocks. Parker tried for a few minutes to keep up with him, but she could hardly get near him without risking serious bodily harm. After a while, she gave up and stalked off. A moment later, Ethan stopped flailing long enough to realize that she was gone. But once he did, he just shrugged and kept dancing. He was sure that this situation would blow over if he just used his Ethan Craft patented method of ignoring the whole thing.

Lizzie, Gordo, and Miranda cracked up. Who needed Ethan and Parker, anyway? In the end, the three of them were the ones having the good time.

it's the three amigos, back together. And i wouldn't have it any other way.

"Hey, guys."

Lizzie looked up to see that Parker was walking toward them. Lizzie's glare was only outdone by Miranda's—who looked like she might try to tear Parker's head off.

"Gordo," Parker said awkwardly. "Can I talk to you?"

"Actually," Gordo said smoothly, pointing to Lizzie and Miranda, "we're talking."

Parker cast a nervous glance at Lizzie and Miranda, then looked back at Gordo. "Listen, I'm really sorry."

Gordo pretended to have no clue as to what she was talking about. "Sorry for what?"

Parker winced. "For calling you short."

"I am short," Gordo pointed out reasonably.

Gordo's back!

Lizzie pointed to Ethan, who was still flapping like a maniac all over the dance floor. "Parker, I think your date is getting kind of lonely," Lizzie said.

"Yeah." Parker's voice was vague—she didn't really seem that interested in Ethan all of a sudden. "Um, listen," she said to Gordo. "Talking to Ethan is kind of like talking to wallpaper. Well, actually, wallpaper's a bit more interesting. Anyway, what I'm trying to say is that I think I came to the dance with the wrong person."

"Really?" Gordo lifted his eyebrows. "'Cause I didn't."

Lizzie couldn't believe how cool Gordo was being—he was ice-cold!

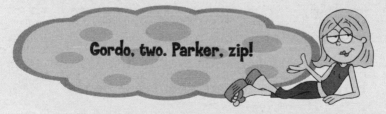

Gordo, two. Parker, zip!

Lizzie grinned and put her arm around Gordo. "I came with exactly who I wanted to," she said.

"Me too," Miranda chimed in.

Parker stood there uncomfortably for a moment. Finally, she asked, "So, um, do you want to dance?"

"Well," Gordo said slowly, glancing at Lizzie and Miranda. "If it's okay with my dates, I guess I could spare you one dance."

Parker looked hopefully from Lizzie to Miranda, then back again.

"Well . . ." Miranda hedged, rolling her eyes.

"I guess it's okay," Lizzie said. After all, Parker had been really brave to come over and apologize to Gordo. Lizzie guessed that deserved some small reward.

Lizzie and Miranda watched as Gordo and Parker walked toward the dance floor.

"I told you he'd come around," Miranda said knowingly.

"Yeah," Lizzie agreed. "For once, Gordo is the one with the problem." She grinned wickedly. "And for once, you get to be right."

Miranda laughed and gave her friend a playful swat on the arm. "Hey!"

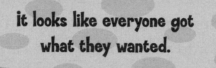

it looks like everyone got what they wanted.

Lizzie watched as Gordo danced with Parker. He looked like he was having a good time.

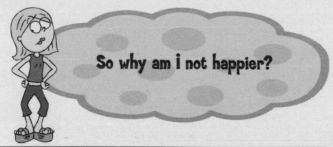

So why am i not happier?

"Look," Miranda said suddenly, "since Ethan's flying solo right now, I'm going to see if I can steal a dance."

Lizzie nodded absently. "Yeah."

"Are you cool?" Miranda asked.

"Yeah," Lizzie lied. She smiled bravely and nodded toward the dance floor.

Miranda hesitated, but finally scurried toward the still thrashing Ethan. But Lizzie wasn't watching him. Her eyes were still glued to where Gordo was dancing with Parker.

"Yeah," Lizzie said quietly, her voice lost in the volume of the dance music. "I'm cool."

Don't close the book on Lizzie yet!
Here's a sneak peek at the next
Lizzie McGuire story. . . .

Freaked Out

Adapted by Alice Alfonsi
Based on the series created by Terri Minsky
Based on a teleplay by Melissa Gould

The freakiest day of Lizzie McGuire's life didn't start out very freaky at all. In fact, it began like any other totally normal school day.

Lizzie got up, brushed her teeth, washed her face, and fixed her hair.

Next came the clothes. Achieving maximum fashion perfection could be a trying process. But that morning Lizzie nailed it in record time. The trick, she found, was first deciding on one piece of clothing, then choosing others to go with it.

This morning she'd started with a silver-studded jean skirt, paired it with a metallic belt, then topped it with a clingy, long-sleeved pink jersey.

Totally stylin', thought Lizzie, checking herself out in the mirror. Then she frowned. There was a small orange spot on the front of her shirt.

Uh-oh, maybe not so stylin'.

She licked her finger and rubbed. But the smudge wouldn't budge.

Just when you think your outfit is perfect, you find last week's pizza stain.

Lizzie examined the stain a bit closer.

Which is kind of weird because it should've been *washed* in last week's *laundry*.

Whatever, thought Lizzie.

She began to rifle through her closet, looking for a new top. But the next one she chose had an ink mark on the sleeve. And the one after that had a juice stain on the collar.

One by one, she jerked the shirts off their hangers. Each one had some sort of disfiguring stain, spot, or wrinkle. And some of her favorite skirts and pants were in the same sorry shape!

Which means something bizarre-o is going on with my wardrobe, and i don't mean my blacks don't match.

This could only be the work of one person, Lizzie realized—her twerpy little rodent-breath brother! With window-rattling rage, she opened her mouth and yelled the dreaded name!

"Ma-a-a-a-tt!"

Then Lizzie stomped out of her bedroom and into the hall.

"You rang?" Matt asked, sliding over to her in his socks.

"What have you done to my clothes?" she demanded.

Matt's eyes opened wide as an innocent little lamb's. "Why, nothing, he said in his

I-have-no-idea-what-you're-talking-about voice.

Lizzie wasn't buying it. She pointed to the pizza stain on her shirt. "Well, then what is this?"

Matt shrugged. "Proof that you're a slob, I guess."

"You are such a vermin!" cried Lizzie. "Why can't you just stay out of my stuff and quit invading my privacy!"

"How is taking your dirty, disgusting, nasty clothes out of the hamper and putting them back in your closet 'invading your privacy'?" asked Matt.

The nerve! "Just stop ruining my life!" she yelled.

"Quit ruining mine!" Matt yelled right back.

Ruining his? thought Lizzie. "What are you talking about?" she asked.

"You never give me my phone messages, you're always taking my lunch to school instead of yours, and you hog the bathroom," said Matt.

"News flash, Matt. You don't *get* any phone messages. And I took your lunch to school *one* time by accident, and I don't hog the bathroom anymore than you do."

Well, maybe a little.

Lizzie threw her hands up. "Fine," she said.

"Fine," Matt shot right back.

In the very next instant, sister and brother cried together, "I'll stay out of your life!"

Then they both turned and went back to their bedrooms, slamming their doors behind them.

Lizzie was so angry, she didn't notice the change right away. But as she stomped further into the room, she realized things weren't quite right.

For starters, she'd just walked *away* from Matt. But now he was standing right in front of her.

Wait! Lizzie thought. That's not Matt. That's a mirror. *I'm* standing in front of it, and *Matt* is staring back.

No. It can't be, she thought.

Slowly, she lifted her hand to her mouth. At the exact same time, the reflection of Matt lifted *its* hand to *its* mouth.

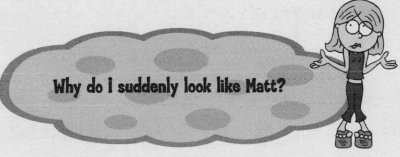

Why do I suddenly look like Matt?

Confused, Lizzie looked around. Action figures, robot toys, and sports equipment cluttered the room.

Hey, wait a minute, she thought. What is this?

This isn't my room!

Lizzie jumped away from the mirror, then back again. But the reflection didn't change. She knew who she was. She was Lizzie McGuire. So why was the mirror reflecting *toad-boy's* face?!

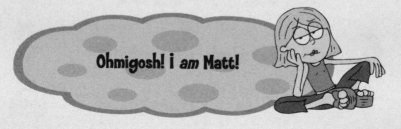

Ohmigosh! i *am* Matt!

Suddenly, Lizzie heard a girl scream in the next room. She ran out of Matt's bedroom and came face-to-face with—*herself*!

"Ahhhhh!" Lizzie and Matt screamed together.

"Kids!" called Mrs. McGuire from downstairs. "Stop your fighting!"

"But I'm you!" cried Lizzie from Matt's body.

"And I'm you!" cried Matt from Lizzie's body.

"Give me back my body, worm!" Lizzie demanded, shaking her . . . well, actually Matt's . . . grubby little finger at her brother, who suddenly looked an awful lot like HERSELF!

"Yeah," said Matt, waving around Lizzie's manicured hand, "like I want to be a stupid girl!"

"Okay," said Lizzie, trying not to panic, "what do we do?!"

"Stop, drop, and roll!" suggested Matt, spinning his, er . . . *Lizzie's* . . . arms to make his point.

"No, Matt, that's fire safety!" said Lizzie. She closed her . . . ummm . . . *Matt's* . . . eyes and tried to remain calm.

Think, she told herself. Just think this through logically. As if *that* were possible.

"How did this happen?" Lizzie asked. But when she spoke, Matt's voice came out. This was way too freaky to comprehend.

"I don't know!" screeched Matt in Lizzie's voice. "One minute I'm switching your shampoo with shaving cream, and the next minute . . . I'm you!"

"But before that, we were fighting," recalled Lizzie.

"We told each other to stay out of our lives, right?" said Matt.

Yes, thought Lizzie, dweeb-boy is right.

"And we said it at the exact same time!" She thought for another moment. "So, let's say it again and see if we switch back," she said. "On my count. One, two, three—"

"Stay out of my life!" they cried together.

For a second, they just stood in the hallway, staring at each other.

"Well?" they asked together.

Lizzie didn't feel any different. She *still* felt like Matt.

Now, what? she wondered, staring into her own face, which was currently occupied by an unwanted guest who seemed to be suddenly distracted by her footwear.

"How high are these shoes?" Matt asked, pointing down at Lizzie's cork-soled mules. "They're kind of cool," he said, teetering a bit as he bent over to take a closer look at them. Then he straightened Lizzie's body to its full height, stretched out Lizzie's arms like

Frankenstein, and began to tramp around. "I am Giant Matt. Fear me!"

"Matt!" screeched Lizzie, horrified. "This is serious!"

As she yelled, Lizzie became aware of something other than the fact that she sounded just like her twerp-boy brother. There was an icky taste in her mouth (well, really *Matt's* mouth). "And when is the last time you brushed your teeth?" she demanded. Her "new set" of chompers felt all slimy and grungy. She picked at them and found a big glob of jelly bean stuck to a molar. "*Yuck.* That's disgusting!"

The phone rang. Lizzie ignored it. "What are we going to do?" she asked her brother. "I *really* don't want to be you!"

"And I really, *really* don't want to be *you!*" said Matt.

Sorry! That's the end of the sneak peek for now. But don't go nuclear! To read the rest, all you have to do is look for the next title in the Lizzie McGuire series—

AT RETAILERS NOW!

Now you can get inside Lizzie's head with great new products!

JOURNALS

FRAMES

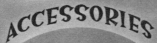
ACCESSORIES

DOLLS

Everyone loves to get
applause

Watch it on

Disney CHANNEL
abc Kids

Visit Lizzie every day at DisneyChannel.com